First published in the United States, Great Britain, Canada, Australia, and New Zealand
in 2014 by NorthSouth Books, Inc., an imprint of NordSüd Verlag AG, CH-8005 Zürich,
Switzerland.

Distributed in the United States by NorthSouth Books Inc., New York 10016.
Library of Congress Cataloging-in-Publication Data is available.
ISBN: 978-0-7358-4164-2 (trade edition)
1 3 5 7 9 • 10 8 6 4 2
Printed in Germany by Grafisches Centrum Cuno GmbH & Co. KG, Calbe,
January 2014.
www.northsouth.com

Brigitte Weninger
Eve Tharlet

Davy
Loves His
Mommy

North
South

The bunny family was enjoying a lunch of carrot stew, but one of the little bunnies was missing.

Suddenly Davy came crashing through the door and shouted, "Boy, oh boy! Am I hungry! Is there anything left?"

"That's no way to behave, Davy!" called Mother Rabbit. "You should say sorry for being late, and have you even washed your paws?"

"Sorry!" said Davy. "But my friends and I were having so much fun. We were guessing who could burp the loudest. Guess who won?"

"Who won? Who won?" asked his siblings excitedly.

"We don't talk about things like that at the dinner table," said Mother Rabbit.

She gave Davy such a stern look that he decided to change the subject.

"Um, when is Mother's Day?" he asked.

"Next Sunday." His mom sighed while clearing the table.

After lunch Max, Lina, Manni, and Mia went out
into the field.

Davy moped along behind them.

"What would Mommy like for Mother's Day?"
his siblings asked.

Little Mia shouted, "A doll!"

"No way!" snorted Manni. "She really wants a pirate ship."

"No, no!" called Lina. ". . . a pretty security blanket."

"Or something nice to nibble on," said big brother Max.

"Wait!" called Davy. "I know what she really wants . . . five well-behaved bunnies!"

"Five well-behaved bunnies? Where are we going to get those?" asked Lina.

Davy laughed. "I mean us! I'm just not sure how yet. . . ."

The siblings were at a loss.

"Oh, I know how!" big brother Max said.

He ran into the house and came back with a big book. "I found this in Dad's book collection. It's called *The Well-Raised Bunny.*"

The bunnies looked at the funny pictures as Max read the chapter names:

"Cleanliness and Tidiness"

"How to Behave at the Table"

"Invitations and Gifts"

"Excusing Yourself Properly."

"Bouncy-beetle-beds!" said Davy. "No bunny can remember this stuff!"

"Of course you can," corrected Lina. "You just need to practice."

"Then let's go to our secret den and practice!" called Davy.

Max was the teacher, as he was the only one who could read. "First of all we all need to have a wash."

"What? Like clean our ears, brush our fur, and clip our claws?" asked Davy, aghast.

Max nodded.

"Okay," said Davy. "But we should save that for later; otherwise Mom will suspect something's up. Read on!"

Next the bunnies practiced behaving at the table.

Lina and Mia brought their tea set, and the three boys picked some raspberries and fetched water.

"Can't I just gobble down the berries from my plate?" sighed Manni.

"'No gobbling or slurping, and no talking with your mouth full'!" Max read aloud. "'No elbows on the table. Don't lick your knife and fork.'"

"What? But that's no fun at all!" Davy complained. "Can't we at least find out who can burp the loudest?"

"NO!" cried Max and Lina together.

Davy sighed again.

Two days later, good behavior was getting easier.
All five bunnies could cut their moss steaks
into small pieces, balance bark chips on
their forks, slice mud pies, and use leaf
napkins.

But then, just as Manni asked
politely, "Can somebody pass me
the sand, please?" Max suddenly
realized: "What are we going to
eat on Mother's Day? We can't
serve sand!"

Davy thought for a while and
said, "I'm going to ask Dad if
he'll help us. And maybe Max
can write a nice invitation."

The next morning there was a knock at the door. But when Mother Rabbit opened it, there was nobody there. Just a pretty pink letter lay on the doorstep.

It read: "Best ever Mother's Day Surprise at 12 p.m. Please wear a pretty dress."

Mother Rabbit wondered to herself, "Who could this be from?"

"No idea," the little bunnies fibbed. "Maybe you should just wait and see."

Finally it was Mother's Day. At 12 p.m. on the dot, a well-scrubbed Davy knocked at the door. He was wearing a bow tie that Lina had made for him.

"Yikes!" cried Mother Rabbit with a shock. "What happened to you?"

But Davy just bowed politely and gave his mom a big bunch of flowers. "Good day, Mom. You are looking wonderful! May we invite you to lunch at the Green Tree Restaurant?"

He took his mom by the arm, and off they walked.

At the edge of the forest they met Davy's soccer rival, Bobby Badger.

"Hey there, little Davy. I always knew you were a mommy's boy!" he taunted.

"Hello, Bobby! We're just on our way to an important appointment; it was very nice to see you again," called Davy politely.

Bobby stared after him openmouthed.

Grandma Squirrel and Mama Badger called out, "Oh, Mrs. Bunny! What a thoughtful and well-raised boy you have."

Davy and his mom winked at each other and smiled.

At the Green Tree, head chef Father Rabbit and his team waited for their guest of honor.

"Welcome, Mom!" they called out.

Lina and Mia took their mom's shawl as Max and Manni sang a little song, and they all sat down to lunch. All five bunny children knew exactly how to behave.

Once Mother Rabbit had finished her dessert she said, "My dear children, what a wonderful surprise. I didn't think you could be so well behaved! Where did you learn so quickly?"

"We taught ourselves." Davy smiled. "Just for you on Mother's Day!"

"Oh, so you're only going to be this well behaved part of the time?"

"Well, it's not as difficult as it seems," Davy admitted with a smile. "Maybe you'll just have to wait and see."